Tooth

and

Claw

Dragon Riders of Osnen Book 7

RICHARD FIERCE

Dragonfire Press

Cover design by germancreative.

Cover art by Rosauro Ugang

ISBN: 978-1-947329-49-2

CONTENTS

1

The wind whipped through my hair.

I closed my eyes and gripped the saddle tightly with my legs, stretching my arms out to the sides. Sion glided smoothly through the sky and I relished the feeling of flying.

Hold on, Sion said, a hint of mischief in her voice.

I blindly grabbed onto the saddle horn, then Sion barrel rolled to the left. My stomach experienced the feeling of weightlessness and leaped with exhilaration. I bit back a scream, clenching my jaw and gripping the saddle so hard I thought I would break it. Sion leveled out only for a moment, long enough for me to open my eyes, then she did a loop. This time I did scream, but it was a whoop of excitement.

"Yeah!"

Demris streaked ahead of us. Maren was astride his back and she waved at me as they passed, her brilliant red hair shimmering in the sunlight. Her beauty was unrivaled. I'm sure that I was biased, but there was something breathtaking about her flying through the sky on her dragon. I felt like I was the luckiest man in the world.

Don't forget about me, Sion said playfully.

I could never forget about you, I replied,

rubbing her neck. *Our minds are so entwined, I think that when I die, I'll still hear your thoughts.*

How poetic. Save those fancy thoughts for Maren.

Sion flapped her wings quicker, trying to catch up to Demris. His head snaked back as if sensing her intent, and he issued a roar, then sped up even faster. Sion tried to get closer to him, her wings beating furiously, but she was no match for him. She gave up and returned to a smooth glide, using the updraft to give her muscles a break.

How much further? Sion asked.

Anesko said the towns were near the foothills of the Gracena Mountains. I've never been there, but I think we're getting close.

A half-hour later, the first of the towns came into view. Based on the map I'd seen before we left the Citadel, there were five towns clustered along the base of the mountains. Though their populations were small, they were responsible for a large portion of the iron ore that flowed into the capital. That was another reason Anesko had asked us to look into the goblin rumors. If there was a disruption to business that affected King Erling, then it needed to be solved as quickly as possible.

I found it ironic that although Maren was no longer considered a princess, she was still technically doing her father's bidding.

I wouldn't mention that to her if I were you, Sion said.

I didn't plan to, I replied, grinning.

Thin plumes of smoke rose from many of the buildings in the town. If I remembered correctly, this one was called Norwich. It was situated on the grassy plains that slowly melded into the hills. A patchwork of farm fields was spread out around the town, and I also spotted some cattle.

Sion hummed in delight, and her desire to eat cow wafted through the bond.

Don't get your hopes up, I told her. *These poor towns don't have enough as it is.*

My words didn't damper her spirit at all. She began her descent, flying slow, wide circles over the town until she dived and landed in the tall grass next to a patch of corn stalks. The golden yellow ears peeked out from their leafy coverings, and I spotted a handful of people moving through the rows, methodically plucking them and tossing them into baskets. It was a reminder that summer was nearing an end.

I climbed out of the saddle and slid down Sion's shoulder, stretching and bending over to work the kinks out of my back. I adjusted my sword belt and looked around for Maren. She was striding toward me, coming from the other side of the cornfield.

"You should be glad we don't bet on these races," she said with a smirk.

"What are you talking about? Sion and I were enjoying the sights."

"I saw her trying to match Demris. You just

can't accept defeat, can you?"

"Maybe you're so competitive, you think people are competing against you even when they aren't." I shrugged. "Besides, it doesn't bother me to lose as much as you think it does."

"I'm just messing with you," Maren said. "You don't have to sulk."

"I'm not sulking. I just don't want to deal with goblins."

"Then why didn't you stay at the Citadel?"

"Anesko sent us both here, remember? I didn't have a choice in the matter."

"So, you don't want to be here with me. Is that what I'm hearing?"

I rolled my eyes. "Don't be dramatic. Of course I do."

"Good. Then let's go find some goblins!"

Maren grabbed my hand and we walked into the town. The main road was hardened dirt, as were the streets in the town, packed down from years of wagon traffic. The ruts in the dirt were a clear indication of that.

All but one of the buildings were single-story structures with thatched roofs, the exception being the brick tavern that stood in the center. Norwich was smaller than anywhere I'd been before, with only two dozen or so buildings scattered along the streets.

"Everything seems peaceful," I said, hoping all

the talk about goblins was just overexcited and mistaken townsfolk.

An elderly woman was walking in our direction, though her attention was on the overfilled bucket of milk she was carrying. She seemed to be struggling with the weight, so I stepped in front of her and smiled.

"Need some help?"

She peered at me suspiciously. "Who are you?"

"I'm Eldwin, and this is Maren. We're dragon riders from the Citadel."

She harrumphed. "So, those are *your* dragons that are causing such a freight with my cows?" She set the bucket down and motioned to it. "It's the least you can do."

I lifted the bucket with my good hand, trying not to splash the milk everywhere. "Where should I take this?" I asked.

"Follow me," the woman said. She continued walking in the direction we'd just come, so I turned and followed her. Maren jogged past me and slowed to a walk next to the woman.

"Have you seen any goblins around here?" Maren asked.

"Goblins? I haven't seen one of those nasty creatures in years. Why do you ask?"

"We've been getting reports that some have been seen in the area. Eldwin and I are here to see if that's true."

"I've not seen any, but my granddaughter just returned from Keth. You can ask her if you'd like, but I doubt she's seen any either. It's been quiet here ever since the king pushed the goblin tribes into the mountains."

Maren looked over her shoulder at me, frowning. She might have been disappointed at the news, but I wasn't. We reached the woman's home, which looked similar to the other buildings. The thatch atop her roof looked like it needed to be replaced, and scrawny chickens pecked at the bare ground in front of the structure.

"Millie!" The woman suddenly shouted, startling me. Milk splashed onto my boots and I stopped walking and held the bucket still. Once the liquid calmed, I carried it the rest of the way to the house.

"Set it there," the woman said, waving.

I assumed she meant near the door, so I gently set the bucket on the ground beside it. As I stood back up, the door opened, and a brown-haired woman stepped out. She was around my age, with bright green eyes and tanned skin. Her clothes were ragged and patched with an assortment of different colored cloths, none of them matching the original garment. Millie stopped short when she saw me, and a huge grin spread across her face.

"Hello stranger," she said.

"Millie, these people are here from the…" she paused and threw her hands up. "They're dragon riders."

Millie's eyes widened. "Truly? I've never seen a dragon up close before."

"Your grandmother mentioned you just returned from another town," Maren said. "Did you see any goblins while you were away?"

"Actually, I did!"

Maren and I exchanged looks.

"Can you tell us about it? Did they attack you on the road?" Maren asked.

"No, nothing like that. There was only one goblin, and it was dead."

"Don't lie to these people, Millie. You didn't see no goblins."

"I did, though!" Millie argued. "Aston said he killed it with his bare hands. Strangled it until it quit moving. He's charging a copper to let people touch it."

"What town was this at?" Maren asked.

"Keth. It's about an hour walk from here, that way." Millie pointed northeast.

"Let's go check it out," Maren said, looking at me. I nodded. Any hope of an easy assignment was now long gone.

"Thank you for your time," I told the older woman. Millie was still grinning at me, and I had the feeling she was a little odd. We left Norwich and headed back to the field where our dragons were.

"She likes you," Maren said.

"Who?"

"Millie."

"I don't think so."

Maren laughed. "She couldn't take her eyes off you. Not that I blame her."

We parted ways at the cornfield, and I mounted Sion.

Goblins? Sion asked.

Unfortunately. There's a dead one in the next town.

Sion stretched her wings and hunched down, then launched herself into the air. She flew low, whipping the tall grass around with each flap of her wings. Demris swiftly caught up to us, but he didn't speed ahead like before. We reached Keth, which was three times the size of Norwich and surrounded by a stone wall. The dragons landed on a hill overlooking the town, and it took Maren and me a few minutes to hike down. Keth was surrounded by a steep moat, though there was no water in it.

The gate was lowered over the trench, providing access to the town. We crossed over it and found a small crowd of people gathered near a tent. I pushed through the press of bodies until I reached the front. Tied to a tall post was the last thing I wanted to see.

2

A goblin.

The spindly creature was dead, but the ropes kept it from falling over. Its skin was a blotchy reddish-yellow hue, but the paleness of death was beginning to take over. A bulky muscled man was standing nearby, holding a small chest with which he collected coins from the crowd. After people paid, he let them touch the goblin.

I didn't understand their fascination with touching it, especially since it could still spread disease even though it was dead. I stepped closer to further inspect the goblin, and the big man shouted at me.

"It's a copper piece to touch it!"

"I don't plan on touching it," I replied, clasping my hands behind my back.

"Looking is free, I suppose," he muttered lowly.

The goblin's eyelids were closed. It was short, maybe four feet in height. I could see bruising around its neck, which led me to believe that the big man had actually strangled it. It wore tattered clothing, made up mostly of animal hides that were sewn together haphazardly. I couldn't tell how old it was, as I wasn't very educated about goblins, but I guessed it was an adult. Its fingernails were grungy with dirt, and they were sharp and pointed.

Maren joined me, standing to my left and peering closely at its face. From my periphery, I saw the big man was watching us. Before I could say something, Maren reached out and lifted one of its eyelids.

"That's a copper piece," the man said, marching over to us. He held out his wooden chest and shook it, the coins inside clinking together.

"I'm not paying you," Maren replied, shooting him an odd look.

"You touched it," he said. "It's my goblin, and I'm charging people to touch it."

Maren stared at me incredulously. I shrugged, then looked at the man.

"My apologies," I said politely. "We should have introduced ourselves. We're dragon riders from the Citadel. I'd like to ask you a few questions about the goblin."

The man's demeanor changed, and he grinned broadly. "My name is Aston," he said. "I'm the blacksmith here in Keth."

"I'm Eldwin." I hooked a thumb to my left. "This is Maren."

"We rarely see riders out here anymore," Aston said. "It's an honor to meet you. I suppose you want to know where I found this little guy?"

"Yes," Maren answered. "Were there others with him?"

Aston closed the lid on his chest and turned to

the crowd. "That's all for today," he said loudly. "Come back tomorrow if you didn't get to touch it yet."

A few people groaned in disappointment, but the crowd dispersed without issue. Once the stragglers were gone, Aston tucked the chest under his massive arm and turned his attention to Maren.

"He was the only one, though there were footprints that told me there were more of them out there somewhere."

"A lot more?" Maren lifted the goblin's eyelid again. Its iris was a solid black circle.

Aston scratched his chin in thought. "Maybe three or four."

"How did you happen upon him?" I asked.

"I was taking some tools to the workers in one of the mines in the hills, and when I was coming back, I saw him. He was alone, and he was armed with a rusty sword. Imagine the little guy's surprise when I grabbed him from behind and choked him."

"So, you *did* strangle him." Maren whistled appreciatively.

"I did, but I hated every second of it. He stunk something foul, worse now that he's dead, and his skin was oily. He almost slipped free, so I had to break his neck."

"Good," Maren said. "These things are evil to the core. If you hadn't killed him, he would have killed you, maybe the miners. Did he seem lost, or was he looking for something?"

"Neither, I don't think," Aston replied. "He was just standing atop the hill, looking at the town. I figured he might be a scout, so a few others and myself went searching the hills. We didn't find anything except some tracks, the ones I mentioned. We followed them, but they didn't lead anywhere."

"Maybe a view from up high will reveal more," Maren suggested, looking at me.

"That's a good idea. I'm sure Sion and Demris will be able to spot the other goblins if they're nearby."

Aston lowered his voice despite the fact no one was around. "Do you think there's trouble?"

"Possibly," Maren said. "Enough reports made it to the Citadel to warrant us being sent here, so I'd say you should probably be ready to evacuate."

I frowned at her response. The last thing we needed to do was cause a panic.

"Just to be safe," Maren added after seeing my expression.

"Yes, just to be safe. Of course." Aston didn't look as relieved as he sounded.

"Don't worry unless we tell you to," I said. "If the goblins are up to something nefarious, they won't be a problem for our dragons."

That seemed to ease Aston's worries. "Have you found somewhere to stay for the night? I know its early in the afternoon, but darkness creeps up early in these parts. You'd probably be better off searching in the morning."

"Not yet," I replied.

"Follow me. I'll show you the best place in Keth. But first, would you mind grabbing the end of the post? I've been carrying this thing by myself, but I wouldn't mind a little help."

I assumed he hadn't noticed my mangled arm. Most people assumed I couldn't do normal tasks, but that was a common misconception. I struggled, of course, but I never used my deformity as an excuse. I nodded.

"Can you hold this?" Aston asked Maren, pulling the chest from under his arm.

She accepted it and Aston grabbed onto the top of the post and heaved upward, his face reddening from the exertion. The end of the post cleared the hole in the ground, and I reached down and lifted it, careful not to touch the goblin. It was surprisingly heavy, which I didn't expect. I fought to get the post up onto my shoulder, but once it was in place, the weight didn't seem as bad.

Aston led us through the town to a small dwelling, where we dropped the goblin off. There was a shack behind the home, and we set the post inside. Aston latched the door, and then he showed us to the local inn. I paid for our room, then we returned to the hill where we'd left Sion and Demris. The dragons were basking in the sun, their wings outstretched.

I'm hungry, Sion complained. *Are we allowed to eat the cows here?*

No, I replied. *I'm sure there are deer or other animals in the hills, though.*

"I think we should at least look around this area," Maren said, motioning to the hills around us. "It's not dark yet, so we can cover some ground now. What do you think?"

"Sure."

We flew over the landscape a few times, but there was nothing out of the ordinary. I spotted some miners heading back to the town and watched them weave their way along the peaks and dips of the foothills. Once they reached the town, we landed back on the hill overlooking Keth and turned in for the night.

Aston hadn't lied when he said it got dark early. The sun quickly disappeared over the horizon. We ate a small meal in the common room of the inn and retired to our room. The bed was comfortable, if a bit small, and we slept until morning light filtered through the window. We washed up using the community basin and had breakfast, then headed up the hill to find Sion and Demris were missing.

Where are you? I asked, pushing the words through the bond. Sion sent me a partial image of a dead mountain lion.

"They're eating," I told Maren.

"I figured as much. Do you think we'll find anything today?"

I shrugged. "I hope that we don't, but when has our luck ever been good?"

We both laughed. In boredom, I picked up some rocks and tossed them down the hill. They tumbled along, clattering against large boulders at the bottom. I heard Sion and Demris approaching and looked to the sky. They were coming from the west, beyond the mines we'd seen the day before.

They landed and we mounted up, then we were off, flying over the hills. We went further out, going north toward the mountains this time. I saw a trail that wound its way through the area, but it eventually faded into the rest of the landscape. It became obvious that the townsfolk didn't normally travel this far into the hills.

I smelled fire in the air and glanced around. Ahead, a plume of gray smoke rose lazily into the sky. I looked at Maren and she met my gaze, nodding to let me know she'd seen it, too. Sion and Demris flew side by side, and they angled toward the smoke in unison. As we got closer, the source of the smoke became clear. A camp with dozens of tents stretched out in a small valley, and I immediately recognized the forms milling around, roughly a few hundred of them.

Goblins.

3

Take us lower, I told Sion.

She tilted to the right and began descending. She didn't get low enough for the goblins to pose much of a threat, but it was low enough that I was able to see more details of the camp. The smoke plume was coming from a fire in the center, where the carcass of a large animal was cooking. It was on a spit, and a group of goblins was turning it over the flames.

The tents were scattered chaotically across the valley, with no semblance of organization to the camp at all. Many of the tents looked like they were about to collapse or fall over. I looked back at Maren and saw that Demris had slowed his pace. She was sitting completely still in the saddle, and I assumed she was in the middle of casting a spell.

A horn blared from the camp below.

I looked down and saw the goblins scrambling. At first, I wasn't sure what they were doing, but then I realized we'd been spotted. Arrows began hurtling toward us, but with a few flaps of her wings, Sion lifted us beyond their range. She circled back and flew beside Demris.

"We should probably get out of here!" I shouted at Maren. "We don't have the element of surprise now!"

She turned toward me, and I noticed the whites

of her eyes were showing. She'd linked her vision to Demris's. I tried to ignore my revulsion.

"This isn't a random gathering!" Maren shouted back.

"Follow me!"

I guided Sion back the way we'd came, keeping a wide berth of the camp, and we landed atop a hill that was flat and large enough for both dragons. Demris dropped beside Sion, stabbing his large claws into the ground to stop his momentum. I dismounted and waited for Maren to join me. I couldn't believe there was an army of goblins out here.

"What did you see?" I asked as Maren slid off Demris's back.

"Nothing good," she replied. "Goblins live in tribes, but not in groups *that* large. I think they are gathering for a reason, and it can't be for anything good."

"Should we go back and evacuate the towns?" I asked. "There's nothing else out here, so I'm sure those creatures must be congregating to launch an attack on them."

"Goblins aren't smart enough to plan anything like that," Maren said. "And rival tribes are always at war with one another." She paused. "If someone has unified them, it can't be good."

"Is that a 'yes' for evacuating, then?"

"No. Not yet, anyway. I think we need to figure

out what they're doing."

"How do you propose we do that?" I asked, then waited for the insanity of her plan.

"We'll need to get inside the camp."

That was about what I had expected her to say, so I wasn't too surprised. "You do realize we probably won't be able to go undetected, right? They'll spot us. And then what? We fight our way out? Call Sion and Demris to come and flame them all? If that's the case, then we may as well have them just do that now."

"Yes, they would probably see us, but that's why we'll go in disguise."

"What do you mean?"

Maren smiled at me. It was the one she used whenever she was going to say something that I knew would get us into trouble. And it was the same one that I always fell for.

"I'll cast an illusion spell that will make us look like goblins. Then, we'll be able to walk around the camp freely without worrying about being seen."

I blinked, momentarily at a loss for words. It was a clever idea to be sure, but it was still risky. "What if you lose focus on the spell?"

"I won't."

"How do you know you won't?"

Maren huffed. "I just won't. Look, we could just send Demris and Sion over there to burn them all to a crisp, but it would be a good idea to know why they are here to begin with. What if there are more of them somewhere else? What if we kill these ones and go back to the Citadel, and then another group of them attack the towns in retribution?"

She made a valid point. I still didn't like the risk involved with her illusion idea, but I didn't have an idea of my own to offer. I looked at Sion, expecting her to side with me.

It sounds like an adventure, Sion said. *You should go.*

I couldn't help but laugh at the ridiculousness of it all.

"I'm not talking you out of this, am I?"

"Not a chance," Maren replied, smiling again.

"How will this work? You'll cast a spell and we'll look like goblins?"

"Exactly."

"We don't speak goblin. Will the spell give us that ability?"

Maren hesitated. "No, it won't. We'll have to refrain from speaking."

I stared at her, hoping she was kidding. She wasn't.

"It's not like we plan to live among them," Maren said. "We just need to figure out what they're doing."

"Well, if we don't speak goblin, how will we do that? I don't think you've got this all figured out."

"Demris knows goblin. He'll listen through the bond and tell me what they're saying."

I thought I'd found a reason for us not to go through with her plan, but it crumbled like sand and blew away.

"Fine, but if things start to go wrong, we're out of there and these two," I pointed to Sion and Demris, "burn the entire camp down."

"That's fair," Maren replied.

"And I'm keeping my sword."

"No problem. I can hide it under the illusion."

It seemed Maren had an answer for everything.

An hour later, Sion and Demris dropped us off within walking distance of the goblin camp. It had taken Maren a while to craft our illusions, but she guaranteed that the amount of detail she put into them would keep us from drawing attention to ourselves.

I lifted my hands and admired Maren's work. My skin was the same mottled color as the goblin from Keth. It was too bad I couldn't fully see myself in a mirror. I was certain I looked terrifying.

We started the trek toward the camp. As we walked, I kept an eye out for scouts. As long as our illusions held up, I doubted we'd have any issues, but I wanted to ensure we had a clear way of escape if something happened. We followed the natural trail that twisted between the hills and, eventually, reached the outskirts of the camp.

Three goblins armed with spears were standing guard as we came around a bend. I tensed, but they barely acknowledged us. I kept my hand on the hilt of my sword, and we walked past them and continued into the camp. Groups of the creatures were gathered near different tents, conversing in their guttural language. Maren had said there were different tribes of goblins, but aside from different shades of skin color, I couldn't tell a difference between them.

"Where are we going?" I whispered.

"To that big tent," Maren replied, nodding toward it. "I saw it earlier. That's probably the leader's and the best place to hear what's being planned."

I stayed beside Maren, glancing around at all the goblins as we walked. It seemed surreal that we were marching around in the middle of an army of goblins. I reached out through the bond and touched Sion's mind. Her presence was comforting and eased my nerves.

I'm close, she said. *If there's trouble, I'll be there quickly.*

That's the main reason I agreed to do this, I replied. *Maren is a capable sorcerer, but our bond is different in a way I can't explain. I trust her, and I trust you, but with you ... it's just different. Does that make any sense?*

No, but humans are odd, Sion said. *I'll grow to understand you fully one day. I hope.* She made a sound that resembled a snicker. I smiled and tried not to laugh. We were drawing closer to the huge tent that towered over the rest. Unlike the others, this one wasn't made of animal skin. It was made of cloth. I glanced at Maren questioningly.

"Maybe they stole it," she whispered.

A hulking goblin was standing near the entrance, much larger than the others I'd seen. He was as tall as I was, with thick flabs of skin showing through his assorted pieces of rusty armor, and he leaned on the end of the shaft of an ax. The bladed end was pressed into the ground under his weight. We walked around to the back of the tent. Thankfully, there were no guards here.

Maren pressed her ear against the tent and listened. I stood near her, keeping an eye out for any unwelcome company. After a few minutes, Maren snapped her fingers to get my attention. I turned to face her.

"There are a few different voices in there, but whoever the leader is asked why dragons flew over the camp. He's afraid his plans have been discovered."

"What are his plans?"

Maren shook her head. "He hasn't said, but whatever they are, he's decided to speed them up. He—" She paused, listening again. "He's telling the others to prepare for something, but Demris doesn't know what the word means."

We stared at one another quietly for a moment. I had an idea, but I didn't know how we'd implement it.

"They can't execute their plans without a leader."

Maren grinned at me. "Let's wait until he's alone. Come on."

We hurried around to the front of the tent, but we steered clear of the guard. The tent flaps opened, and five goblins stepped out. They looked different than the others, but they weren't as large as the guard. They wore necklaces of teeth, ears, and other body parts.

"Those are chieftains," Maren said.

"What about the big one? The guard?"

"That's a hobgoblin."

The chieftains dispersed to different parts of the camp, leaving the leader by himself. We were about to sneak back around the tent when he stepped out. Maren sucked in a breath, and I felt my heart drop into my stomach.

It was the sorcerer from Tiradale.

4

"Impossible," Maren whispered.

"Please tell me I'm seeing things," I said.

"If you are, then I am."

The sorcerer walked to the center of the camp and stood near the fire. He pulled his hood back, and there was no mistaking it. The black hair, the hawkish nose. It *was* him. He spoke, his words booming across the camp, but he was speaking in the goblin tongue. The rasping, throaty words echoed off the surrounding hills.

"He's using magic," Maren said.

"Well, I didn't think he spoke that loud normally."

"No. I mean, yes, he is projecting his voice, but he's using other magic, too. It's the same slippery magic from Tiradale. He must have another flute."

"There's something else," I said. "He's able to talk. Didn't Giffor say he removed the man's tongue?"

"You're right," Maren replied. "I'd forgotten about that." She frowned. "Giffor must have released him, but why?"

"I don't think he'd do that. The man kidnapped his daughter, after all. He must've escaped. The real mystery is how is he talking without his tongue?

Can magic restore body parts like that?"

Maren shook her head. I quieted as the sorcerer continued speaking. The camp was hushed, the creatures enthralled by his every word. When he finished speaking, a cheer rose from the goblins, driving them into a frenzy. They began chanting and lifting their weapons into the air.

"What did he say?" I asked.

"He's summoned more tribes, and they have answered his call. They're coming down from the mountains."

"We need to warn the towns and help them evacuate," I said.

"It's too late for that. We already know the goblins have scouts out there. If they get wind that the people are fleeing …" She let the words hang in the air.

The goblins had formed into small groups and continued their chanting.

"We need to do something," I said. "I'm calling Sion."

"No!" Maren clasped my hand. "We can stop this."

"How?"

"We'll capture the sorcerer. Without a head, the snake can't see."

"But it can still move," I argued.

Maren stared at me in silence for a moment,

then pushed past me and ran toward the tent. The sorcerer was watching his army, not paying attention to us. I muttered a curse and sprinted after Maren. She reached the tent and the hobgoblin stepped in front of her path, lifting his ax and hurling a string of gravelly words at her. I drew my sword and lunged at him, driving the blade between an opening in his armor. The sword plunged into his stomach, and he went down with a gurgled cry of surprise.

I looked back to see if we'd drawn attention, but his cry must've been drowned in the tumult of the other goblins. I wiped the blade on his tattered pant leg and sheathed it. Maren helped me pull him into the tent, and we dropped him to the side. I grabbed the edge of a rug and pulled it over him, then we moved to opposite sides of the entrance and waited.

My heart was thundering in my ears. This was insane. If something went wrong, we'd be dead before Sion and Demris could get to us. My mind swirled with horrifying possibilities, and I reached out for Sion. Something was blocking our connection. It was dark and empty, like some kind of void.

Sion?

There was no reply. I tried to navigate around the darkness, but it was everywhere. It sucked in all of the words and feelings I tried to convey to Sion, forcing them into the void. I looked at Maren, confusion starting to give way to panic. Before I could say anything, the sorcerer stepped inside the tent. He walked to a table covered with a map.

Small figurines were scattered across its surface. Maren lifted her hand, drawing my attention. She had three fingers up, then two, then one.

"I know you're there," the sorcerer said.

Maren paused mid-step, and I grabbed the hilt of my sword. The man didn't move.

"Your illusion is good, but it's not perfect," he continued. "Who are you? And why are you here?" His tone was calm and collected as if he wasn't the least bit concerned about us. He moved one of the figurines, then turned around, his gaze sweeping past me and landing on Maren.

"Wait. Let me guess … those dragons belong to you two, don't they?"

"Don't act like you don't recognize us," Maren said.

"Should I?" He whispered something under his breath, and our illusions faded. I drew my sword and took a step forward.

"I wouldn't do that if I were you," he said, his eyes flicking over at me momentarily.

"How did you escape?" I demanded. "The baron isn't going to spare your life this time."

The sorcerer's brow furrowed. "I truly have no idea what you're talking about. I will ask one final time. Why are you here?"

"He's lying," Maren said.

"I know," I replied.

"Suit yourselves." The sorcerer began chanting the words to a spell. Maren also cast a spell, and she completed hers before he did. A blast of invisible force knocked the man backward. He struck the table and tumbled over it, falling to the ground. The map and figurines went flying in all directions. Maren rushed forward and put her boot against the sorcerer's neck.

I joined her, pressing my blade against the palm of his left hand.

"How did you escape?" I repeated.

"Fools," he rasped. Maren's foot was cutting off his airway, his breaths coming in strained wheezes.

"Maybe he was tortured to the point he doesn't remember anything?" I suggested.

"No, he's lying. And I can prove it."

"How?" I asked, glancing at the entrance. The clamor of the goblins outside hadn't subdued, but I didn't want any of them walking in and surprising us.

"The dragon bone flute," Maren answered. "Check inside his robes."

I knelt beside him, setting my sword down, and patted his chest and sides. Something solid was on his left side. I pulled his robes open and saw the edge of the white flute peeking out from a pocket. As I reached for it, the man tried to say something, but Maren pressed her foot down harder, cutting off his words. He struggled against her, his entire body jostling about. I managed to grab ahold of the flute.

"Hold still!" Maren snapped.

The sorcerer's free hand swung up from the ground, striking the back of Maren's leg—the one holding her weight. Her leg involuntarily bent, and she toppled backward with a cry of surprise. The man sat up and hit me in the throat. I choked and released the flute, my hands going to my neck. My eyes watered, blurring my vision.

I saw Maren's vague outline moving, and the two began struggling. I fought to inhale, adrenaline making my vision pulse. I blinked rapidly, clearing the tears from my eyes. Maren was trying to grab the flute from the sorcerer, but he was stronger and faster. He smacked her hand away and scrambled backward. I finally got air into my lungs and reached for my sword, clutching the hilt weakly. In desperation, I tried to call out to Sion.

The darkness was still blocking our bond, and I had a feeling it had something to do with the sorcerer. I staggered to my feet and swung sloppily, my balance off-center. I missed, and the sword went flying from my grasp, clattering somewhere behind me. I cursed my weak hand and turned to look for it.

The sorcerer chanted, firing off a spell. I threw myself to the ground and rolled over, looking for the danger. Whatever he'd cast hadn't been meant for me, but Maren must have countered it. She was unharmed and in the middle of casting her own spell. I scrambled on my hands and knees and spotted my sword lying nearby. I crawled over and snatched it up, then stood and rushed the sorcerer.

My grip was firmer this time, and I swung horizontally, trying to score a hit across his ribs.

My blade landed, tearing a long cut through the robes, but the victory was short-lived. The robes hung in the air for a moment, then collapsed to the ground. The sorcerer was gone. I whirled around, expecting an attack from behind. He wasn't there.

"Where is he?" I asked.

"He's gone," Maren replied. "He used a teleportation spell."

"Blast it!" I struck the fallen table with my sword. "We need to get out of here and warn the towns. Can you reach Demris?"

There was a pause, then she shook her head. "No. Something is blocking the bond."

"I'm having the same problem. I guess we'll have to flee on foot. Maybe if we go north, we can circle back to where Sion and Demris are."

Maren nodded, but she seemed troubled.

"I'm sure they're fine," I said, though I wasn't sure I believed the words myself. When we'd encountered the sorcerer's magic before, it had caused all kinds of issues with our dragons. I assumed this was the same situation.

"It's not just that," Maren said. "I—"

A horn blared, followed by goblins pouring into the tent.

5

I pushed Maren behind me and turned to face the creatures.

They swarmed through the entrance, their ranks growing thicker by the second. I stepped forward and swung my sword, hacking an arm off the nearest goblin. It shrieked and grabbed at the stump, trying vainly to stop the bleeding. I kicked him out of the way and struck another one in the neck. My sword got stuck, but I jerked it free just in time to block a rusty sword from impaling me.

I parried the blade to the side, sending the goblin's arm out wide, then planted my foot on his chest and kicked him backward while using the momentum to push myself away from more swinging blades. A goblin with a mace came at me, screaming murder. I ducked low and jabbed the tip of my sword into its knee. The creature crashed into my shoulder, dropping his weapon and flipping over my back. It landed hard on the ground behind me. I grabbed the fallen mace and came up quickly, swinging the weapon in an underhanded fashion.

It connected with another goblin's jaw, cracking its head back with a loud snap. The goblin collapsed, tripping up two others. They tumbled to the ground at my feet, and I swiftly plunged my sword into their backs, one at a time. Another goblin rushed at me, swinging its sword wildly. I blocked the strike, the goblin's rusty blade glancing off my cross-guard, and launched a counter-attack with the mace. The weapon collided with the side of the goblin's head, resulting in a crunch that made me flinch.

In the back of my mind, I wondered why Maren hadn't cast any spells. Perhaps she had, and I just hadn't noticed. I pushed the thought away and tried to jerk the mace back, but it was pulled from my grasp as the dead goblin fell. The others held back, none of them willing to engage me. My sword lessons at the Citadel had paid off. I was breathing heavily, but I still had plenty of strength. It was doubtful I could cut our way out of here, but Maren could obliterate them all with a single spell.

I changed hands, tossing the sword to my other hand, then ran my right hand along my pants, wiping the sweat off. It was in that moment three goblins swiftly ran at me. I grabbed the hilt of my sword with both hands and swung as hard as I could. The first one went down as I severed its head from its body. I struck the second one, but my blade bounced off its pauldron and tremors ran along my arm. I leaped backward as the third one tried to jab me with a spear, and I managed to twist my sword around and chop the iron tip off.

One of the goblins shouted, their voice booming over the noise. The crowd of goblins parted, revealing one of the chieftains. He snarled something and took a step toward me. I raised my sword and leveled it at him. The goblin looked at the blade, then repeated what he'd said. I stared at him blankly. Did he expect me to surr—

Maren screamed.

I whirled around. Two goblins had grabbed her arms. She struggled against them, but more joined the fray and they subdued her, knocking her down. I raised my sword, but a piercing noise filled the air, sending a sharp pain through my head. I dropped my sword and covered my ears, but it didn't help. The sound reverberated through every part of my being, forcing me to my knees.

And then a host of goblins overcame me. They punched and kicked me, but surprisingly didn't stab me. Their blows hurt, but the piercing noise was worse. Finally, blessedly, the sound faded. The goblins jerked me to my feet and bound my arms behind my back. I looked for Maren and saw they had tied her up as well. The goblins forced us into the corner, and they went about clearing the bodies from the tent. Once their work was done, they left us alone. I looked at Maren.

"Are you hurt?" I asked.

She shook her head.

"That's good. I still can't reach Sion. It must be that blasted sorcerer's magic again."

"I don't think it is," Maren said softly.

"What do you mean?"

"I didn't want to say anything until I knew for sure, but … I think something is happening to magic. At first, I thought it was just me. When I cast certain spells, they don't always work. And if they do, they quickly fail."

I thought back to when we'd battled the basilisk. Maren had used a containment spell on the creature, but it had fizzled out. I shook my head.

"No, that can't be it. There's one thing connecting Tiradale and this place, and it's the sorcerer. It has to be that flute he's got."

"Eldwin." Maren turned her head toward me. "I noticed it first at the Citadel a few weeks ago. When we went to Tiradale, it was worse, but it started before that."

I didn't believe it. She had to be wrong. Perhaps she was just focusing too hard and overthinking things. How could something be wrong with magic? If there was a problem, surely Sion would … *No, I* thought. I considered her illness in Tiradale, the void in our bond now. Could it be true?

"Have you spoken to Anesko about it?"

"No."

"You should. If there truly is something happening with magic, I'm sure he's aware of it."

"Unless we find a way out of here, I don't think it's going to matter," Maren said.

I struggled against the ropes the goblins tied me with, but they were too tight. I checked the ground for my sword. It was gone. One of the goblins must have taken it. Blasted creatures.

The tent flaps opened, and I snapped my head toward the entrance to see who it was. The sorcerer stepped inside and glanced down at his ruined rug.

He *tsked* and turned his attention to us.

"Now, then. Where were we before you rudely attacked me? Ah, yes. You were just about to tell me why you are here." He strode across the tent and stopped a few feet away.

"Why do you think?" Maren snapped. "Your army of goblins was reported to the Citadel."

"I figured they might draw unwanted attention before I was ready, but it was a risk I was willing to take. Goblins are dumb and expendable. I can always find more."

"We know you're planning to attack the towns. Why? They're poor. What is there to gain?"

"I don't owe you an explanation," the sorcerer said. "But since we're all here and no one is going anywhere, why not?" He clasped his arms behind his back. "Where shall I start? From the beginning, I suppose."

The man was calm, too calm. We'd attacked him, and instead of killing us, he was calmly talking to us. It didn't make sense, but then, none of it did.

"When I was a child, I grew up in Keth. My brother and I helped our parents with their crops, and life was … simple. When we turned ten, however, things changed. We were able to feel magic. Being young and untrained, we played with it." The man smiled, his eyes staring off.

"We taught ourselves many spells, but we didn't know what we were doing, or what we had. And neither did the people who shunned us as beings of darkness."

"They banished you?" I asked.

"Not at first, no. They made my family suffer and starve, hoping it would force my parents into leaving the town. They were poor, as the girl aptly mentioned, and couldn't go anywhere. They took our land away and refused to sell anything to us."

I was starting to see where this was going.

"They offered my parents a proposition. Kill us and they would restore everything to them. I will admit that they tried. My parents led us into the hills, to this very valley. It was my father who convinced my mother that it was the only way to get their lives back. He was like the other people in the town. Afraid. Afraid of what they do not know."

"Your parents tried to kill you?"

"Just so," the sorcerer said. "I killed my father first. I told myself it was *he* who was evil, and I burned him alive. My brother was more sadistic than I, and he … well, suffice it to say that my mother's death was much more brutal."

"You and your brother were the same age?" I asked. "That would mean—"

"Twins," he said, cutting me off. "Yes, we were twins. I haven't seen my brother in years, but now I know why you thought you recognized me." His stare became intense, his eyes shifting from me to Maren and back.

"Tell me, where is my brother?"

6

"He's rotting in a dungeon," Maren growled. "The same as you will."

The sorcerer laughed. "In case you haven't noticed, I'm the one with the power here. I could have you both tortured to death with a single word."

Maren glared at the man, but she didn't say anything else.

"Yet, I will show you both mercy. Once I've razed those pathetic towns, you'll be free to go."

"If you hurt those people, I'll make sure you face justice," Maren said.

"You're funny, girl. You can barely get your spells to work. How do you expect to overpower me?"

"My spells work just fine," Maren replied.

"Oh? Then show me. Cast one right now."

I glanced at Maren from my periphery. She stared stone-faced at the sorcerer, but she didn't make any attempt to use her magic.

"There's a reason I didn't gag you," he said. "And it's the same reason you haven't freed yourself yet. The only reason some of your spells worked is because you were in my vicinity."

I considered what Maren had said about magic failing. The sorcerer seemed to know about it as well, which worried me. Maren's expression softened somewhat, but she still looked imposing.

"What's happening to magic?" I asked.

The sorcerer turned his attention to me. "No one is really certain, but it's affecting everyone magically inclined. I wouldn't be surprised if your dragons start acting erratically."

There must have been a change in my expression because the sorcerer smiled knowingly. "Ah, so you've already noticed it, have you? It's not surprising really. Dragons are highly attuned to magic. They probably noticed the change before we humans did."

I reached out through the bond again, but the void was still there.

"Why isn't your magic affected? You teleported out of here with no problem."

"Oh, it's been affected, but there are workarounds to the problem."

"It's the flute," I said, realization dawning on me.

"Very astute," the sorcerer said. "You are correct. The flute is carved from the bones of a dragon and enhanced with runes. It aids in centering the magic, but it isn't a cure to the problem. Eventually, it too will stop working."

A horn blared, and the sorcerer smiled. "More tribes have arrived. Well, as I said, I'll free you as soon as I'm done with the towns. Until then …" He offered a mock bow, spun around, and left the tent.

"We need to get out of here," I said, turning to Maren. "Is your magic working?"

"No," she replied glumly.

More horns blared, followed by the sound of marching feet. The noise eventually faded, and I knew that time was running short. Innocent people were going to die if we couldn't find a way to warn the towns. I struggled against the ropes again, but they didn't loosen.

The tent flaps opened and a goblin peeked inside. He stared at us for a moment, then left. I'd assumed the creatures had all gone to attack the towns, but some had been left behind, likely to guard the camp. I heard footsteps behind me, but they were on the other side of the tent. It was probably another goblin walking the perimeter.

"Psst!"

I looked at Maren, but she was looking around curiously.

"Was that you?" I asked.

"No. It came from over there somewhere." Maren nodded toward the tent wall.

I peered past Maren and watched. A hand slipped under the tent, but it wasn't the hand of a goblin. The cloth lifted and a human head appeared. It was the girl from Norwich, Millie. She smiled broadly and crawled into the tent.

"There are so many goblins out there," she said

cheerily.

"That's a bad thing," I replied. "Can you untie us?"

"I sure can!"

Millie walked behind us and untied the ropes holding me, then she and I worked on Maren's bonds. Once Maren was free, I hurried over to the entrance and peered out, spotting a handful of goblins talking amongst themselves.

"How did you end up here?" Maren asked.

"Ever since Aston found that goblin, I've been exploring the hills trying to find more. I came across your dragons, and when I saw you weren't with them, I kept going until I saw this camp. You two are lucky I found you!"

I walked over to the sorcerer's desk and spotted my sword propped against the back of it. I snatched it up, then looked at Maren and Millie.

"We need to get to the towns and warn them. The goblins are headed their way now."

"How do we get there in time? I still can't reach Demris."

I tested the bond and finally felt Sion's presence.

Thank the gods! Are you all right?

I'm a little weak, Sion said.

Can you fly? We need to alert the townsfolk of the goblins. They're marching toward the towns as we speak.

Yes, I can fly. I'm on my way.

"Sion's coming," I said. "She'll take us to Keth."

"There's three of us," Maren said. "That's a lot to carry."

"I'll stay behind," Millie said.

"It's too dangerous," Maren replied. "You and Eldwin can go, and I'll stay here until I can reach Demris."

"No. I know my way around these hills better than anyone. Besides, as much as I like the idea of riding a dragon, I don't think I'm ready for that."

Maren and I exchanged looks. I shrugged, leaving it up to Maren. I didn't want to leave either of them behind, but if Maren's magic was still unreliable, then I'd rather she go with me so I could make sure she was safe.

"Fine," Maren surprisingly relented. "We better hurry. The goblins have a head start."

"There are a few guards outside that need to be dealt with," I said. "Stay in here."

Before Maren could argue, I ran out of the tent. The goblins were standing in a circle, and when one of them spotted me, he issued a loud *whoop*. The others turned to face me and brought their weapons to bear.

I ran straight for them. Their circle opened up and I was in their midst, suddenly surrounded.

Perhaps I'd been a little too hasty. The nearest goblin swung its sword at me. I brought my blade up, knocking the strike aside, then thrust forward. The goblin's midsection was bare, and my sword sliced into the exposed flesh. It screamed in agony and fell to the ground.

Another of the creatures jabbed a spear at me, but I dodged the blow and cut the spear in half. Without any hesitation, the goblin leaped at me, slamming the blunt end of one piece into my head. My vision burst with a thousand stars and I staggered backward, bumping into another goblin. It jumped on my back and bit into my shoulder with its jagged teeth.

Searing pain tore through my flesh. I slammed my head back, cracking skulls with the goblin. It released me and fell, tripping me. I tumbled to the ground and dropped my sword, but quickly recovered and stood back up. The goblins tightened their circle around me. Sliding my foot under my sword, I kicked it up and grabbed it in mid-air, then launched myself into a spin. I extended my arm as I whirled about, my sword cutting down two of the goblins.

A wave of dizziness swept over me. I stood still, waiting for it to fade. The remaining goblins took advantage of my momentary lapse and rushed me. I ducked and darted to the side, the ground seeming to tilt under my feet. The whizzing sound of blades cleaving the air behind me sent a chill up my spine.

I spotted Maren at the tent entrance, staring out at me. It was too bad her magic was acting up. I could really use the help. Turning back to face the goblins, I barely brought my blade up in time to block a sword strike. Our weapons clanged together, stunning the goblin. I brought the hilt of my blade into its face, crunching its nose and sending the skinny goblin crashing to the ground.

A roar filled the air.

I smiled knowing Sion was almost here. Her presence emboldened me, and I launched myself at one of the goblins, slashing diagonally and cutting it from shoulder to waist. The last few goblins turned and fled as Sion swooped low and landed nearby.

Move, she said, inhaling a deep breath. I sprinted out of the way and she opened her jaws, spewing a stream of flames that engulfed the fleeing goblins. One of them crashed into a tent, setting it aflame. The other two continued running up the hillside, but they slipped and rolled back down, thumping against large rocks. When their limp bodies came to a halt, they didn't get up.

Where's Demris? I asked.

He's ill, but he will come when he recovers.

Maren and Millie came out of the tent and joined us.

Can you carry all three of us?

Sion snorted. *Not if you want to get anywhere quickly.*

It was worth asking, I replied with a grin.

"Ladies first," I said to Maren.

She climbed up into the saddle, leaving space for me to sit in front of her. I scaled Sion's shoulder and settled myself, then looked at Millie.

"Find somewhere safe to stay until we can get rid of the goblins," I said. "Maybe the mines?"

"I know a few places," Millie replied, smiling at me. The look in her eyes reminded me of what Maren had said, how she thought Millie liked me, but there was only one woman who held my heart.

"Good. Stay there until you hear the fighting stop."

Take us to Keth, I told Sion.

She launched into the air.

7

We sped south. The landscape below us whizzed by quickly, and it was hard to discern anything other than blurred colors. Sion grew tired and eased her pace, but I soon spotted the unruly goblin army.

This should slow them down, Sion said. She flew low as we passed over the creatures, breathing fire among their ranks. The smell of scorched flesh hit my nostrils and I tried not to gag. With a few flaps of her wings, Sion lifted us higher and we continued toward Keth. I looked back and saw the march of the goblins had temporarily stopped.

That bought us some time, but I'm not sure it will be enough.

Let them come, Sion replied. *I'll flame them all.*

Keth came into view, its thin stone wall the only thing that stood in the way of the approaching army. Sion descended and landed outside the town near the bridge that spanned the defensive trench. I leaped from the saddle and hit the ground running.

"Get inside the town!" I shouted as I sprinted over the bridge. "Goblins are coming!"

The townsfolk nearby gave me odd looks, but they carried on with their tasks, ignoring my warning. A group of men was loading a wagon with ore, and I stopped when I reached them.

"I need your help," I said breathlessly. "We need to get everyone behind these walls. Goblins are coming from the hills."

The men exchanged glances with each other, then one started laughing. That caused the others to do the same.

"That's a good one! You almost had me there," one of the men said.

"It's not a joke. They're heading here right now."

"Sure they are," the man replied.

The others continued chuckling as they worked. I spun around, looking for Aston. The big man wasn't showing off his goblin trophy, so I headed for his smithy. It was a short square building across from his home. I flung the door open and rushed inside without thinking. A wave of heat struck me, and I spotted Aston pounding a large hammer against a rod of glowing hot metal.

Aston looked up from his work and offered a friendly nod. It was so hot inside the place that I was already felt sweat forming on my brow. I maneuvered my way through his shop and motioned for him. He tossed the smoldering rod into a bucket of water and it sizzled and steamed.

"What's going on?" Aston asked. "You look troubled."

"Troubled doesn't even come close," I huffed. "There's an entire army of goblins approaching from the north. We need to warn everyone and close the gates."

Aston set his hammer down and pulled off his gloves. "An army of the buggers, you say? So the one I found *was* a scout."

"Yes. People aren't listening to me, though. We don't have much time."

"I'll get the mayor," Aston said. "Come with me in case he has questions." The big man paused, then grabbed his hammer. "Just in case I need it." He smirked.

Aston hurried out of the smithy, and I followed quickly on his heels. He went straight to the inn, which I found odd, but inside we found the mayor of Keth. He was an older man, with thin gray hair and a long handlebar mustache. He was enjoying a tankard of ale at the bar as he chatted with the barkeep.

"We've got a problem, Godwin," Aston said as we joined him at the bar.

Godwin licked his lips and set his tankard down. "Is this about our earlier discussion?"

"I'm afraid so. The dragon rider says there's an army of the creatures headed here now."

Godwin sighed and rose from his stool. "Twenty years of peace was a good run, I suppose." He grabbed the tankard and downed what remained, then slammed it down on the bar. "Sound the alarm. I'll meet you at the gates."

"Where are you going?" Aston asked.

"To get my sword," Godwin replied. "It's probably buried under a foot of dust."

A bell began tolling outside.

"Looks like someone beat you to it," Godwin said.

Aston and I left the inn and I spotted Maren at the bell tower. It wasn't anything impressive, just an upraised platform with a bell hung overhead on a pole. Maren was pulling the rope affixed to it and a small crowd was gathering.

"Stop that racket!" someone shouted. "That's for emergencies only!"

"It is an emergency!" Aston bellowed to be heard over the clanging. "Goblins are coming! Prepare to raise the bridge!"

The men I'd spoken to earlier were there and their apparent leader glanced at me uneasily. "Apologies," he said. "We had no idea you were being serious."

"I told you I was," I snapped.

"What about the other towns?" a woman asked. "Have they been warned? I have family in Norwich."

Aston pointed at the group of men. "I hope you can run fast," he said. "You've been chosen as messengers."

The leader sputtered, but the other men nodded and rushed off without question. Aston glared at the man until he threw his hands up in defeat and followed after the others.

"Will they make it in time?" I asked. "How far are the other towns from here?"

"We're all spaced a couple of miles apart," Aston said. "Keth is the closest to the hills, so hopefully we can keep the attention centered here."

I noticed he hadn't answered my question, but I didn't press him further. Sion and I could have flown to the other cities, but I knew we were needed here more. People began rushing in from the farm fields.

"What about the miners?" I asked.

"With any luck, the goblins will pass right by the mines. The workers stay there until the evening, so they should be safe. As safe as can be, anyway."

Maren stopped ringing the bell and stepped off the platform.

"I can feel Demris through the bond," she said.

"Is he coming here?" I asked.

"No. He's not feeling well, so he's staying put for now."

I could see the worry in her eyes. I felt it, too, but we had more pressing matters to deal with before we could start delving into the problem with magic.

"Can you use your magic?"

"I think so," Maren answered. "I can feel it like normal right now."

"Tell your dragon to come inside the walls once everyone else has entered. There's no need for her to be out there when the goblins arrive."

I nodded and conveyed the message to Sion.

They're getting close, she said. *I can smell their stench in the air.*

The wall surrounding Keth was tall but thinner than typical. I hoped that the goblins didn't get the bright idea of rolling boulders down the hills. If they did, I was certain they'd smash through the weak defenses.

"Is there a way for you to request help from the Citadel?" Aston asked.

"Yes, Maren could send word magically to our master, but there's no one available to help. Given recent events, our riders are scattered too thin as it is. We're on our own."

Aston grunted, his expression grim. "At least we've got a dragon and a wizard to help."

I admired that he was looking on the bright side of things, but I had my doubts. That blasted sorcerer had an advantage over Maren with the flute, but I prayed she would be able to out magic him.

A handful of people crossed the bridge into the town. Aston looked to the west wall and waved at a man who'd taken position there.

"Are the fields clear?"

"Just about," the man called back. "There's a few more coming around to the gate!"

"Where do you want me?" I asked.

"Wherever you think you'll be most useful," Aston replied. "We should be safe behind the walls, so I don't expect too much trouble unless the goblins figure out how to climb over."

I knew Aston was putting too much trust in the strength of the walls, but I didn't want him to share my doubts so I kept my mouth shut.

"I'm going to help close the gates," Aston said. He jogged away and I looked at Maren.

"What's the plan?" I asked.

"I think I'll stand atop the wall near the gate so I have an open view of the goblins. I assume they'll come straight for the gates. The closer they are, the more damage I can do."

"Sion will be able to breathe fire over the walls. My main concern is the sorcerer."

"That's mine, too," Maren said. "I just hope my magic doesn't falter."

"It's too bad you didn't bring the flute we found in Tiradale," I replied. "It would be really handy right now. Let's get up top."

We found a wooden ladder near the gate that gave us access to the top of the wall. There wasn't a rampart near the gate, so we perched precariously on top of the wall itself. I glanced down at the ground and my heart leaped within my chest. If one of us fell, it wouldn't be pretty.

The bridge began to rise and the chains clinked

loudly. Sion flapped her wings and cleared the wall, landing behind the bridge as it slammed shut. Someone shouted a warning, and I looked toward the hills.

The goblins had arrived.

8

They came swarming down the hills, a wave of spindly red bodies.

Sion stood on her hind legs and breathed a gout of flame over the gate. The inferno struck a group of goblins who were racing for the trench. Their bodies succumbed to the fire and withered like parchment being burned. My stomach churned with disgust, but I managed to steel myself against the revulsion. Now was not the time for weakness.

The rest of the army reached the bottom of the hills and charged ahead. Two groups formed, splitting down the middle, and they rushed into the trench. I watched in confusion, unsure of what they were doing. A couple of them slipped as they traversed down the sloped ditch, falling and getting trampled to death by their fellows.

"They're up to something," Maren said.

"Yes, but what?"

"There's no telling, but we don't need to wait and find out."

Maren stretched her right hand out over the wall, grabbing ahold of me with her other one. She chanted the words to a spell and I was relieved to see her magic work. A small cloud formed in the air below her hand. It was dark and flickered with light, reminding me of a storm. Droplets began falling onto the goblins below, and their screams filled the air.

"Acid cloud," Maren said proudly.

"Clever."

I surveyed the hills, looking for the sorcerer, but he was strangely absent. Sion sent another blast of flame into the goblin ranks. On the opposite side of the gate, Aston and a few other men were firing arrows at a group of the creatures in the trench. The goblins were pressing themselves close to the wall, but whatever they were doing was being hindered by the rain of projectiles. More goblins rushed in, lifting shields over their heads to defend themselves.

"Such stupid creatures," Maren said. "They're being slaughtered, yet they keep coming."

"I'm sure they're under the sorcerer's spell. He'll sacrifice every last one of them to get his revenge."

"I almost feel bad for them," Maren replied. "Almost."

She unleashed another spell. Hundreds of green glowing orbs materialized in the air, and with a flick of her wrist, Maren sent them hurtling out across the field. Everywhere they landed, tiny explosions popped off, blasting holes both in the ground and in unlucky goblins. I'd seen Maren cast much more powerful spells before, and I assumed she was holding back for her encounter with the sorcerer. There was still no sign of the man, which started to worry me.

He's out there, Sion said. *I can feel his flute pooling magic around him. The pull is strong, but I've put up a barrier to protect myself.*

Is the flute trying to pull magic away from you?

Yes, Sion replied. *It's a wicked instrument.*

Another horde of goblins entered the trench and started climbing atop the shoulders of their fellows. I realized what they were doing.

"They're trying to scale the wall," I said to Maren.

"I've got these ones handled," she replied. "Go warn Aston."

I left my position on the wall and rushed to the other side of the gate, swiftly climbing up the ladder. Aston fired off an arrow, then cursed as it glanced off a shield.

"They're climbing on top of each other to get over the wall," I said.

"That's what I was afraid of. We can't hit the blasted things because of their shields. Any ideas?"

I glanced around the town and spotted the wagon filled with ore. "How heavy is that stuff?" I asked, pointing.

Aston grinned. "They've got some weight to them." He issued an order to have the wagon brought to the wall. A crowd of townsfolk helped push the wagon into position, and then they formed a line, hefting chunks of ore from the wagon and passing them along. A basket attached to a rope allowed Aston and the others to pull the ore up, where they began throwing the pieces over the wall.

Despite their shields, the heavy chunks of stone crashed into the goblins, sending them tumbling and destroying their living ladder. I grabbed one of the stones and tossed it down, striking a prone goblin in the leg. It howled in pain and tried to crawl away, but another stone collided with its head, knocking it unconscious.

"That was a brilliant idea," Aston said, clapping me on the shoulder.

"Don't get too excited yet," I replied. "The sorcerer still hasn't shown his face."

A horn blared in the distance and we all turned to look. From this distance, it was hard to see anything. A long odd-looking spyglass was affixed to the wall and Aston looked through it, swiveling it about.

"Speak of the demon and he shall appear," Aston said. "You might want to see this."

We exchanged places and I pressed my eye to the end of the device. Atop a hill, surrounded by the goblin chieftains, stood the sorcerer. He was staring down at the town, his arms folded across his chest. Other goblins were appearing on the ridgeline, rolling large boulders into place.

"These walls aren't going to hold up against that," I said, straightening.

"Hold up against what?" Aston looked again. His face paled.

"Is there anything we can place against the walls to—"

The words died in my throat as the sky lit up and an explosion erupted at the gate. I experienced the sensation of flying before landing hard on my back, the air forced from my lungs. My ears were ringing, and I started to panic when I couldn't breathe. I struggled for what felt like a long while, but finally, I gasped in a deep lungful of air. I caught my breath and rolled onto my hands and knees. Sion was gone, and chaos was all around me.

A great hole had been blown into the gate, and goblins were starting to enter through it. I got to my feet and drew my sword, the movement sending sharp lances of pain down my spine. I hoped I hadn't broken anything in my fall. I rushed forward, meeting the first goblin and removing his head from his body with a single strike. Blood splattered the gate behind him, small rivulets dripping down onto the heads of the other goblins pushing their way through the hole.

Aston appeared beside me with two other men. They were armed with swords and we easily kept the goblins at bay. The hole was large enough for the creatures to scramble through, but they could only come in one at a time.

"What was that?" I asked, stabbing a goblin in the chest.

"That sorcerer sent a bolt of lightning into the gate," Aston replied. "I nearly fell with you, but I was able to grab onto the edge of the rampart. Are you all right?"

"I think so," I replied. The pain wasn't as sharp now, but it still hurt to swing my blade.

Where'd you go? I asked Sion.

I'm on the other side of the wall, she replied. *I'm afraid to flame the goblins this close without damaging the wall, so I'm stepping on them.* Her mirth flooded the bond. *They crunch.*

Something struck the wall and the ground trembled beneath my feet.

Let me guess, that was a boulder, I said.

Yes.

There was another thud, followed by another. I looked up to see Maren holding onto the wall for support as she braced herself against the concussive thuds.

"The rocks are rolling into the trench!" Maren shouted.

"At least they aren't smashing the wall to pieces!" I yelled up at her.

"No, but they're filling the trench! One more in the center and they'll have a walkway to the gate!"

Can you move the boulders out of the trench? I asked Sion.

I don't think so. My strength hasn't fully returned yet. There was a pause. *More goblins are coming down from the hills.*

The ground trembled again. At least the goblins

had stopped coming through the hole. For now.

Are you in front of the gate? Sion asked.

Yes.

You might want to move. There's a boulder rolling toward it.

"Get out of the way!" I shouted, then rushed off to the side.

"It's about to get bloody!" Maren shouted.

I watched the gate and waited. Time seemed to stand still. My heartbeat drummed in my ears. Droplets of sweat collected on my forehead, and I brushed them off with the back of my hand. Everyone seemed frozen in place, waiting to see what happened. The roar of the boulder rolling across the ground filled the air.

There was a clatter as stone struck stone, followed by a crunching sound. Then the gate splintered into pieces and the boulder came tumbling through the debris. It rolled into the town and crashed into a building before coming to a stop.

I looked back at where the gate had been. There was nothing left of it. I spotted the boulders in the trench and saw the horde of goblins rushing toward the opening. Terrified screams filled the air behind me. They pushed me inexplicably forward. I tightened my grip on the hilt of my sword and looked up at Maren.

She met my gaze and nodded knowingly. This was it. This was the last chance to stop the creatures and save these people. I turned back toward the gate and readied my sword.

9

Aston and a few others joined me, standing side by side to form a line in front of the ruined gate. The goblins did a wobbly dance over the boulders and crossed the threshold, throwing themselves at us.

We were outnumbered, but we were stronger and more organized than the goblin ranks. Although these people were miners and farmers, they fought with all they could muster because they had everything to lose. The area quickly spiraled into chaos with the sheer number of goblins, but Maren's spells blasted down among the horde and gave us a small advantage. I cut down two goblins, then blocked a third from impaling Aston with a spear.

He offered a quick nod of thanks before driving his blade into the chest of a goblin that had somehow dropped its weapon. The ground was already wet with blood, and the goblins continued to run across the bridge of boulders.

We could use some help over here, I told Sion.

As if conjured by magic, Sion's sleek form passed in front of the ruined gate, her fire scorching a multitude of the creatures that had yet to reach the trench. They collapsed, their screams of pain causing their fellows to pause. I prayed they would give up and flee, that their fear would overpower the sorcerer's magic.

My hopes were dashed as the goblins lifted their weapons and shouted in their guttural language, charging ahead. Sion leaped back and forth in front of the gate, breathing fire and stomping on any goblin that got in her way. Despite Maren's magic and Sion's flames, there were still many more goblins to fight.

I slashed and stabbed, working my muscles beyond their limits. The pain in my back was buried under the burning in my arms and the cramps in my core. My grip was weakening on the hilt of my sword, but I couldn't take a break. There was no one to fill my spot, and a few of the townsfolk had been cut down. Our thin line of defense was on the verge of breaking.

From my periphery, I saw Maren magically float down off the wall. She landed past the trench and sprinted away from the town. Where was she going? Was she retreating? No, that wasn't like her. Searing pain erupted above my elbow, and I hissed in an agonized breath. A goblin had scored a hit with its rusty sword.

I thrust my blade forward, stabbing the goblin in the eye. The creature fell backward, dead before it crashed into the mass behind it. The other goblins shoved its body out of the way, fighting to take its spot in the thick of the action.

The sky lit up with a brilliant light, causing a lull in the battle as we all looked for the source. Out on the field, Maren and the sorcerer had engaged in a magical clash. I took advantage of the momentary surprise by striking down three more goblins. The lull broke, and the chaos continued anew.

I wanted to be out there with Maren, even though I knew there was nothing I could do against a sorcerer. I was worried about her, and it was hindering my ability to focus on deflecting blows. The sharp tip of a spear barely missed striking the left side of my face. Air ruffled my hair as it shot past, and I knelt in the dirt, jabbing my sword into the creature's exposed thigh. It howled in pain, and Aston slammed his hammer into its jaw, silencing it forever.

"Thanks!" I shouted.

"Now, we're even!" He grinned.

Every muscle in my body seemed to be screaming at me, and sweat dripped freely down my forehead. I risked a glance along our line and saw that a third of the men had fallen. Many of them were dead, but a few were crawling behind the line, moving away from the battle, leaving behind trails of blood.

A jagged bolt of lightning cracked down from the darkening sky, blasting into the ground where Maren and the sorcerer were. The sorcerer's magic must have been affecting the weather, for gray clouds had filled the heavens. I kicked the nearest goblin, sending him reeling into a small group behind him. They all tumbled off the edge of the trench, crashing into the boulders and falling into the ditch.

Something's happening, Sion said.

What?

Something with the magic. The flute is pulling a great amount of magic to the sorcerer.

My thoughts turned back to Maren, my concern growing. She seemed to be holding her own against the sorcerer, but who could know what he was capable of? A glowing barrier formed around Maren and the sorcerer hurled several spells at her. The barrier blocked them all.

"Watch out!" Aston cried.

I looked around for danger, but it wasn't me he was warning. I spotted Godwin, the town's mayor. He was splattered with blood, and some of it was his own. His arms were covered with nicks and gashes, but otherwise, he seemed unharmed. He rotated his sword up, blocking a strike, then grabbed a goblin by the wrist and jerked it forward, impaling the creature through the stomach.

"We can't take much more," Godwin huffed.

And then I noticed that some of the goblins had started retreating. Most of them continued to cross the makeshift bridge, but here and there, a few turned and fled back to the hills.

"He's losing his power," I said. "The sorcerer's control over the goblins is weakening!"

I assumed it was because his focus was on Maren, but I also considered the issue with the magic. Perhaps his flute wasn't as powerful a tool as he believed.

"Close the gaps!" I shouted. "Move forward together!"

Those who remained followed my command, and we moved forward as a cohesive unit, closing the openings between us. We were all covered in blood, and the exhaustion was evident on every man's face. They pushed ahead anyway, and we drove the goblins back, step by step.

The ground trembled as the sorcerer cast a spell, and the enchantment over the goblins was broken. They blinked and looked around as if waking from slumber. Aston roared and lifted his hammer over his head. The goblins scattered, tripping over each other as they rushed to escape. Their numbers were considerably lower now, but they still could have taken the city if they wanted to. Cowards by nature, they fled back to the hills.

Sion flamed some of them as they passed her, but she didn't pursue them.

Can you help Maren? I asked her.

No. My shield is gone and I feel my strength ebbing away.

I started to leave the town, but Aston put his hand on my shoulder.

"You should stay here," he said. "Unless you've got magic also?"

"No," I replied, shaking my head. He was right, I should stay, but I couldn't bear the thought that there was nothing I could do to help Maren. I chewed on my lower lip as I watched the two battle it out with spells, all while the remaining goblins bolted across the field around them.

Bright flashes from each of them lit up the landscape, temporarily blinding me. As my vision returned, I saw Maren's barrier ripple and fade. A haunting tune filled the air, and I realized the sorcerer was using his flute. Sion started to roar, but it ended up as a choking sound and she collapsed to the ground.

"Sion!"

I pulled away from Aston and rushed out to her, tripping and rolling into the trench. My fall was broken by a pile of goblin bodies, their vacant eyes staring off into the distance. One of them was a chieftain, his necklace of teeth and ears pulled tight against his neck. I tried not to stare at them as I stepped over their lifeless forms, half crawling up the trench wall. I reached the top and ran to Sion.

Her presence was absent in the bond. The void that had blocked our connection earlier had returned. I stroked the scales on her face, once again feeling helpless. Sion's eyelids were closed, but her body moved up and down with her breathing. That was a good sign. I looked over my shoulder at Maren.

She'd summoned another barrier, and the sorcerer's spells cracked and boomed around her, fizzling from existence when they touched the glowing shield. The sorcerer rushed her, swinging his flute and striking her barrier. It cracked like glass and shattered into pieces that floated away and dissipated. The sorcerer played the flute again, and Maren dropped to her knees. She covered her ears, and a shiver ran along my spine as I remembered how the tune had affected me.

I stood, gripping the hilt of my sword tightly. He would probably kill me, but I couldn't let him hurt Maren. I took a few steps toward them, but exhaustion had taken its toll. My legs quivered with weakness and my sword slipped out of my hand, the tip driving into the ground. Maren screamed. The sorcerer was standing over her, playing his flute with one hand. In the other, he was holding a mace.

"Gods, no," I whispered.

A massive silhouette took shape in the clouds above them, and I could only wonder at what the sorcerer had conjured now. An earth-shattering roar pierced the air. The sorcerer turned to look. The clouds parted, and Demris's green form came streaking down.

10

The sorcerer swung his mace, but it bounced off Demris's scales and the dragon snapped the sorcerer up in his jaws. He chomped, then flung the man aside. I wanted to run to Maren, but my muscles only allowed for a slow walk. By the time I reached her, she was standing near the sorcerer's body. Demris was behind her, his head peering over her.

"Are you all right?" I asked.

"I will be," Maren replied. She looked as tired as I felt.

The sorcerer was lying on his back, his eyes gazing up at the sky. Demris's teeth had ripped holes in his robes, and a puddle of blood had formed under him. A wheezing sound escaped his lips, and I realized he was still alive. Barely.

"He's suffering," I said, glancing at Maren.

"As he should," she replied calmly. "This is his just reward."

We stared at him in silence, and after a few more breaths, the sorcerer died. I felt like I should do or say something, but I didn't know what. I grabbed Maren's hand and pulled her close, hugging her tightly.

"You did it," I said. "You saved the town."

"Well, you helped a little," she laughed.

I rolled my eyes at her. We trekked across the field back to town. Sion was conscious again, and she nuzzled me as I wrapped my arms around her snout.

You had me worried again, I told her.

Worry gives small things big shadows. I'm fine.

How does the magic feel now that the sorcerer isn't mucking around with it?

It's better, Sion said.

Good. I rubbed the scales on her neck and she hummed in response. I turned to Maren.

"What about his flute?"

"It's broken," she said. "Probably from Demris's attack."

I nodded. At least one of those instruments was gone now. My body was begging for rest, and Maren and I headed into Keth. Aston and Godwin were near the ruined gate, tossing goblin bodies into the trench.

"We are in your debt," Godwin said. "Anything you need, ask and it's yours."

"I need sleep," I replied.

"You still have your room at the inn," Aston said. "It's on us, so don't worry about paying for another night."

"Thank you, but that's not necessary," Maren said. "We're just doing our duty."

"And we're just honoring you for your service,"

Godwin smiled. "Please, go and rest. I do ask one favor, though."

Maren raised her brow quizzically. "Yes?"

"Come and speak with me before you leave."

"Consider it done," Maren said.

We left them to their work and headed to the inn. After cleaning ourselves, we went to our room and found a platter of food waiting for us. I ate a little and then fell asleep in the bed. When I awoke, it was still daylight. I'd only been out for a few hours, but Maren was still asleep. I quietly left the room and went outside to find Aston.

He was working with Godwin and a few others. They had cleared the goblin corpses from the town and were preparing to burn them in the trench. The boulders had been cleared from it, and I assumed Sion and Demris were responsible for that. Another group was out in the field, dragging the remaining corpses there to a small mound that had already been formed of the creatures.

"How can I help?" I asked.

"You've done plenty," Godwin answered.

"I don't mind. Really."

"Well, if you insist, you can help me with repairing the gate," Aston said.

"Just tell me what to do."

Aston and I went to his workshop and began cutting boards and attaching them with steel bands. We built small sections and carried them to the entrance, then laid them out and connected them all. We worked for hours, and Maren eventually came out and aided with the work. By nightfall, most of the gate was assembled. We enjoyed a small feast with the rest of the townsfolk, all of whom poured out their thanks to us.

We retired to our room late in the evening, and the next morning we prepared to return to the Citadel. I offered Aston my help with the gate again, but he was adamant that we'd done more than anyone could ask for.

"Where can we find Godwin?" I asked.

"His place was destroyed by the boulder that rolled into the town, so he's staying at one of the empty homes near the rear wall," Aston replied.

Maren and I found the building easily enough, and I knocked upon the door. It opened a moment later and Godwin smiled at us.

"Come in," he urged.

We stepped inside and took a seat at a table where Godwin had been working. Parchments and other items covered its surface, and Godwin slid them aside.

"Thank you for coming to see me, and thank you again for everything you've done. I know that some of the people here didn't believe that goblins would ever attack us again, and I hope they've learned a powerful lesson."

"Nothing is ever certain," Maren said.

"Except death," Godwin replied.

"True."

"The reason I wanted to speak with you is a little unorthodox." Godwin shifted in his chair and ran a hand through his greasy hair.

"Speak your mind," I said.

"The man behind all of this … I went to the field to look at him yesterday. He was pretty mangled by your dragon, but I recognized him. He grew up out here among us."

"We heard the details while he had us as his prisoners," Maren said. "Is it true his parents were forced into trying to kill him and his brother?"

Godwin sighed. It was true. I could tell by his demeanor.

"Yes, it's true. I had nothing to do with that, though. I wasn't mayor at that time. Back then, I'd just moved out here to work the mines. It was a guaranteed job, and my career as a sellsword wasn't going very well."

"But you knew about it?" Maren asked.

"Sort of. A lot has changed since then. The old town leadership kept things how they wanted, without regard to the others living here. Needless to say, after the bodies of the parents were found, the people in power were thrown out of town. We never saw those twin boys again, and I always wondered what happened to them."

"They killed their parents," I said. "From what

he told us, it sounded like they split ways at some point. The odd thing is, we encountered his brother in Tiradale a few weeks ago."

"Truly?" Godwin leaned forward. "The world can be a small place. How is he?"

"He's in a dungeon," Maren answered before I could.

"Oh." Godwin's expression turned downcast. "I'm sorry to hear that."

"Both brothers turned out to be monsters," Maren said. "The other one was turning people into stone with a basilisk and selling the statues."

The color drained from Godwin's face. He grabbed a wooden cup from the table and took a sip.

"There's something else, isn't there?" Maren asked.

"Yes. I have a daughter who is like you."

"Assertive and strong-willed?" I asked with a chuckle.

Godwin smiled. "That, too, but I meant that she's a sorcerer. At least, I think she is. Her mother passed away a few years ago, and she wasn't a magic user, so I've got no idea how she birthed a daughter with the ability. Anyway, she can do things that don't seem normal. I was hoping that maybe you could take her to the Citadel. She needs proper training. While the people here are more open-minded then they used to be, I'd rather not have another situation as those boys had."

"Well, unless she wants to be a dragon rider, the Citadel won't be able to train her," Maren said. "It's a school for dragon riders. Magic is a small part of it, but it sounds like she needs to learn from a true sorcerer."

"Is there a school for sorcerers?" Godwin asked.

"Not one like the Citadel, but there are places where she can tutor under someone who knows what they are doing. I can speak with someone that should be able to train her. He takes a few apprentices twice a year. I'll send word to you to confirm, but I don't see any reason why your daughter wouldn't be able to join him in the fall when he takes on his next group."

"Thank you," Godwin said. "You've both been a blessing to Keth, and now to me personally. I will never forget your deeds."

"We're just—"

"Doing your duty," Godwin interrupted Maren. "I know. That doesn't mean you can't accept gratitude, does it?"

"Of course not," I replied. "We'll accept it, but we won't bask in it."

"As I said," Maren continued, "I'll send word to you. In the meantime, if you see any more goblins, make sure to let us know. We don't want another horde marching down on you."

"I trust that between you and your dragons, we won't see any more of those blasted creatures for quite some time."

We all shared a smile, and then something occurred to me.

"There was a girl from Norwich that helped us. Her name is Millie. Do you know her?"

"I do," Godwin said.

"Has she been seen? She refused to ride on Sion when we came to alert Keth about the goblins."

"I saw her earlier this morning actually. She wanted to see the sorcerer, but his body had already been burned."

I sighed in relief. "I'm glad to know she's safe."

"I'll let her know you asked about her when I see her again."

"Thank you."

"Well, I don't want to keep you any longer than I already have," Godwin said, rising from his chair.

Maren and I also rose, and we followed him to the door and left.

"I hate to admit it," I said, "but I'm glad we came here."

"So am I," Maren replied.

11

Our trip back to the Citadel was uneventful.

Sion and Demris both seemed weary, but they didn't complain. We boarded them in the stable below the school, then worked on our report for Master Anesko. He was strangely absent, and no one could tell us where he had gone. Given the intense nature of the events at Keth, Maren and I wrote our report in the library for a change of pace. Maren did the writing, while I chimed in with details.

After we finished, I searched through the library's cabinet for anything related to dragon bone magic. As I expected, there wasn't even a topic for it, nor was there anything closely related. It bugged me that the twin brothers had somehow crafted those flutes on their own. I didn't want one, but I did want to know how they were made. Perhaps if I could figure that out, I could also find a way to combat them.

"What are you doing?" Maren asked, joining me.

"I'm trying to find resources on magic involving dragon bones, but there's nothing here."

"I wouldn't expect there to be. When a dragon dies, their bones are buried in a sacred place and left undisturbed."

"I know," I replied. "Which is why I don't

understand how those two got their hands on any. They would've had to know where a burial site was."

"That, or they got the bones from somewhere else. Maybe someone like the people who had Sion when you first found her?"

"I hadn't considered that," I admitted. "I'm surprised the Order never did anything about those kinds of people."

"If they had, you'd never have bonded with Sion."

"That's true. I suppose things have a way of working themselves out sometimes." I paused, thinking about the brothers again. "The sorcerer said he hadn't seen his brother in years. Do you think they created the flutes at the same time?"

"What do you mean?" Maren asked.

"Well, if they got those bones from someone, what are the chances that they did so *after* they separated and went their own ways?"

Maren frowned. "Maybe the brother in Tiradale was lying when he said he made it. If he got it from someone, and his brother got one as well, we might be looking at some sort of black market organization."

"That's what I was thinking," I said. "I don't want to consider how these people are getting dragon bones if they aren't stealing them from burial sites."

We stood in silence for a moment before I closed the drawer I'd been searching through.

"Is it dinner time yet?" I asked.

"Have you heard the bell chime yet?"

"No."

"Then no," Maren replied.

"I wonder where Anesko went?" I changed the subject. "He practically never leaves the school."

"It is curious, isn't it? Maybe he went to meet with the other masters. Now that they're focused on rebuilding, I'm sure there's a lot to consider."

We left the library and waited outside the dining hall until the thirteenth bell signaled dinner. Maren and I ate our fill of smoked salmon, fresh bread, and cheese. I expected Anesko to arrive before curfew, but as the last bell sounded, he still hadn't returned. Maren snuck down to the stables to be with Demris, but I retired to our room. Considering our recent promotion, I was certain nobody cared that Maren didn't abide by the curfew. Not that she followed the rules, anyway.

In the morning, I was awakened by the first bell. Since it was still dark, and I was exhausted, I went back to sleep until the second bell. The extra hour was just what I needed. I got out of bed and went to the bathing chamber to clean up. After I washed, I looked over the wound on my arm in a mirror. I'd kept it covered, but it was still sore and inflamed.

A first-year student entered the chamber and

nodded at me, then paused as he saw what I was doing.

"That's a nasty gash," he said. "Have you been to the infirmary?"

"Not yet," I replied. "If it doesn't look any better tomorrow, I'll have it checked."

Feeling clean and refreshed, I returned to my room and found Maren was awake. She was dressed and practically tackled me when I walked in.

"Guess what?" she asked.

"What?"

"I said guess."

I shrugged. "Are they serving ham at breakfast again?"

"No. Anesko is back!"

"Good. Did anyone figure out where he went?"

"Not that I know of. He sent a messenger to tell me that he wants our report as soon as possible. I was just waiting for you."

"I'm ready," I replied, grabbing the pile of parchments from the desk we shared.

When we reached Anesko's door, the Curates were filing out of his chamber. We waited until they were gone before stepping inside. I put the report on his desk and slid it across to him, then took a seat.

"Are you all right?" Anesko asked, looking at me.

"Yes. Why?"

"Your bandage is bloody."

I looked down at my arm and saw he was right. The wound must have opened back up.

"It's nothing," I said.

"Have it looked at," Anesko said. His tone indicated that it wasn't a suggestion.

"Where were you?" Maren asked.

"I was away on business," Anesko answered vaguely. "Seeing how many pages are here, I take it the goblins were more than just a rumor?"

"A lot more," I replied.

"Yeah," Maren agreed. "And your mind is probably going to have trouble believing everything that happened."

Anesko flipped through the pages quickly, speed reading over the account. His brow rose, and he said, "Twins. Interesting."

He straightened the pile and pushed it aside. "It sounds like you two are heroes."

"I wouldn't use that term," I said.

"Don't listen to him," Maren quipped. "We almost died, so I think the term hero is perfect."

"I'm glad that you both are alive and well. In the future, send a request for aid."

"We had it covered," Maren said.

"This time, maybe," Anesko replied. "The risk

you took was too big. Many lives could have been lost. I'm disappointed in your lack of good judgment."

"What would you have done?" I asked, genuinely curious. "We're stretched thin as it is."

"I would have diverted some riders to assist you," Anesko replied. "We're all busy, but an army of goblins being controlled by an insane sorcerer takes precedence."

"Understood," I said. "It won't happen again."

"I trust that it won't."

The conversation felt like it was over, and I was about to stand when Maren spoke.

"The sorcerer said that magic is being affected by something."

There was a long pause. As it stretched on, it became apparent that Anesko knew something. He had a troubled look on his face, and he seemed hesitant to say anything.

"I'm concerned about our dragons," I said. "When we were in Tiradale, I assumed their illness stemmed from the magic of the flute. The timing lined up. And then again in Keth. Only this time, it wasn't just a momentary weakness. There was a void that blocked my bond with Sion. I couldn't feel her presence or anything."

"Shut my door," Anesko said lowly.

I did as he asked and returned to my chair.

"Some things are happening, but we don't know

what the source is."

"What do you mean when you say that? What types of things are happening?" Maren asked.

"Spells are feeble or don't work at all. The connection between riders and dragons are starting to become unstable. There are other things as well, but I don't want to worry you."

"That's why you left, isn't it?" Maren asked. "Your 'business' was looking into this."

"Yes."

"What about the other schools? Are they reporting the same things?"

"I haven't heard from the other masters in a few weeks, but I would assume so. I've received reports from mage guilds all over Osnen. The king has his sorcerers investigating the matter as well."

"It's happening everywhere," I muttered.

"That's safe to say. As I said, I don't want you to worry. We're doing everything we can to find out what's causing it, but it's going to take some time. Effective immediately, all riders are being recalled to the Citadel. Until we can figure this out, I don't want anyone out there."

"What if there's an emergency?" Maren asked. "What if the goblins return to Keth?"

"I'll make decisions on a case by case basis," Anesko replied. "I won't leave people defenseless if that's what you're worried about, but I also won't risk the lives of riders or dragons either."

"How would it be a risk to send us somewhere?" I asked.

"Imagine you're flying when your bond fails, and your dragon goes unconscious. A fall from that height would kill anyone."

That mental image gave me pause. I hadn't considered anything like that happening.

"That's a sobering thought," I said. "Are there any theories as to the cause?"

"Plenty of them to go around," Anesko answered. "None of them are grounded with any proof, though." Anesko rolled his neck and rubbed his eyes. "I haven't slept in two days, so I'm going to rest. You're dismissed."

Maren and I rose from our chairs and left the room. As we walked along the hall, I glanced over at Maren. There was a determined look on her face, and it was one I knew well.

"What are you thinking?" I asked.

She looked at me, a mischievous grin pulling at her lips.

"Do you really want to know?"

12

Maren refused to say anything until we got to our room, which led me to believe that whatever she had planned was likely going to get us into trouble. At this point in our friendship, I all but expected it anyway.

"Do you find it odd that Anesko hasn't heard from the other masters in a few weeks?"

I shrugged. "Maybe a little, but since Anesko said that magic is being affected everywhere, I assume the other masters have problems of their own to deal with."

"I don't think so," Maren replied. "Magic is crumbling around us. I think the reason he hasn't heard from them is that the lines of magical communication are down. What if they are in trouble and no one knows?"

"That could be possible," I agreed. "But what can we do about it? Your magic fails half the time, and our dragons are being impacted a lot harder than we are. I keep thinking about what Anesko said. What if someone is in the air when their dragon gets ill?" I shook my head. "That's not something I want to experience."

"Neither do I, but I don't like being in the dark. What if one of the other schools has figured out a way to deal with the problem?"

"What exactly *is* the problem?" I asked. "I

mean, I understand the gist of it, but what is it like for you? I don't really know how to explain what I want to say."

"The flow of magic is normally like a river. It's constant, always flowing. Lately, it's more like a wave. It comes and goes. Sometimes there's plenty of it, and other times it's as if it doesn't even exist."

It was hard for me to relate, as I had only cast a single spell, but the way the magic felt as it flowed through me was not something I would ever forget. If that was what Maren felt all the time, then I could see how odd it would be for it to suddenly be absent.

"What do you want to do?"

"I want to go to the other schools," Maren answered. "If you don't want to come with me, I understand. You can stay here and—"

"I'm going with you," I interrupted. "There are too many things that could go wrong, especially if you are alone. I think it's best if we go together."

"I wouldn't be alone," Maren replied. "I'll have Demris."

"Until he gets ill again. I'm not worried about Anesko getting upset with us for leaving, but I *am* concerned about something happening if you go alone."

"I'm not trying to tell you to stay, silly," Maren smiled. "I want you to come."

"When do you want to leave?"

"Tonight."

"I figured as much," I said. "Well, since Valgaard is as cold as living in a block of ice, we're going to need something warm to wear. I'll see what I can find. I assume we're going there first?"

Maren nodded. "Yes. We'll get Hrodin out of the way, then see Katori. I like Hrodin less than you do, so the less time we have to spend around him, the better."

"Thank the gods," I muttered. "I'll gather what we need and start putting it in Sion's stable. What about the guards?"

"Let me worry about them," Maren said, grinning.

"Fine by me. Just don't hurt anyone."

Maren snorted. "I'm not going to do anything like that. They'll just ... take a nap."

The rest of the day was comprised of me hovering around the dining hall and finding opportune times to sneak our supplies down to the stable. Sion and Demris seemed rested and in good spirits, and I prayed they would stay that way.

Subconsciously, I avoided the Curates and Master Anesko. I felt a little guilty about what we were planning, but it was for the good of everyone. If we could find something that would help, that was all that mattered. I wasn't excited about seeing Hrodin again, but that couldn't be helped.

By the time evening came and the curfew bell

rang out, I was more than ready to be on our way. We waited for another hour, just to be certain there were no stragglers, then we used the hidden door in the women's bathing chamber to get into the stable. Maren snuck off to the entrance while I saddled Sion and Demris.

"All is well," she said, returning a moment later. "The guards should be out long enough for us to get well away from here."

I handed Maren a pack filled with food, along with a thick winter robe made of deerskin. The magical collar that allowed Sion to shift into a human was tucked into the saddle, and I went through a quick mental checklist.

"I think we're all set," I said lowly.

"Good. I'll go first. Wait a few minutes to follow me, just in case."

Maren walked Demris up to the entrance, then climbed into the saddle. With a *whoosh* of air, the two disappeared into the night sky. I waited as she asked, anxiously playing with the hilt of my sword.

Demris says it's all clear, Sion told me.

Let's go.

I climbed into the saddle and laid low so I didn't hit my head on the cave ceiling. Sion took us out of the stable, and I sat up straight and glanced around the courtyard. It was quiet. The two guards on duty were slumped against the wall, their game of dice unfinished.

"Good night, gentlemen," I whispered.

Sion launched herself into the sky. The air was cool, but it felt good against my skin. Sion angled upward, flying higher until we spotted Demris's silhouette. We flew beside him, turning west toward Valgaard.

For once, I was actually looking forward to leaving the Citadel. Perhaps it was the fact that we had a higher purpose in mind, a problem bigger than our own petty needs to solve. Whatever the reason, I was ready for the challenge ahead.

THE END

ABOUT THE AUTHOR

Richard Fierce is a fantasy and space opera author. He's been writing since childhood, but began publishing in 2007. Since then, he's written multiple novels and short stories.

In 2000, Richard won Poet of the Year for his poem *The Darkness*. He's also one of the creative brains behind the Allatoona Book Festival, a literary event in Acworth, Georgia.

A recovering retail worker, he now works in the tech industry when he's not busy writing.

He's married and has three step-daughters (pray for him), three dogs (huskies!), three cats, two ferrets and a fish. He basically has a zoo.

His love affair with fantasy was born in high school when a friend's mother gave him a copy of *Dragons of Spring Dawning* by Margaret Weis and Tracy Hickman.